Asterix in Spain

Gaul was divided into three parts.
No, four parts—for one small village of
indomitable Gauls still held out against the
Roman invaders . . .

Asterix and Obelix are engaged in returning
a young Roman hostage to his home in Spain.
As always they leave their mark wherever
they go.
'The puns, allusions and funny names shower
as richly as ever.'
Audrey Laski in *The Listener*

TEXT BY GOSCINNY

Asterix in Spain

DRAWINGS BY UDERZO

Translated by Anthea Bell and

Derek Hockridge

KNIGHT BOOKS
Hodder & Stoughton

ISBN 0 340 19103 1
Copyright © 1969 Dargaud Editeur
English-language text copyright © 1971 Hodder & Stoughton Limited
First published in Great Britain in 1971 by Brockhampton Press Ltd
This edition first published in 1974 by Knight, the paperback division
of Brockhampton Press Ltd (now Hodder & Stoughton Children's Books),
Salisbury Road, Leicester
Third impression 1976

Printed and bound in Great Britain by
Richard Clay (The Chaucer Press) Ltd, Bungay, Suffolk

GAULISH VILLAGE

COMPENDIUM

LAUDANUM

AQUARIUM

TOTORUM

ARMORICA

BELGICA

LUTETIA

GAVL
[ROMAN
CONQUEST
50 B.C.]

CELTICA

PROVINCIA

AQUITANIA

The year is 50 BC. Gaul is entirely occupied
by the Romans. Well, not entirely. . .
One small village of indomitable Gauls still
holds out against the invaders. And life is not easy for the
Roman legionaries who garrison the fortified camps of
Totorum, Aquarium, Laudanum and Compendium . . .

Now turn the book sideways
and read on . . .

a few of the Gauls

Asterix, the hero of these adventures. A shrewd, cunning little warrior, all perilous missions are immediately entrusted to him. Asterix gets his superhuman strength from the magic potion brewed by the druid Getafix.

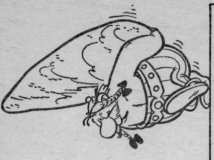

Obelix, Asterix's inseparable friend. A menhir delivery-man by trade, addicted to wild boar. Obelix is always ready to drop everything and go off on a new adventure with Asterix—so long as there's a wild boar to eat, and plenty of fighting.

Getafix, the venerable village druid. Gathers mistletoe and brews magic potions. His speciality is the potion which gives the drinker superhuman strength. But Getafix also has other recipes up his sleeve....

Finally, Vitalstatistix, the chief of the tribe. Majestic, brave and hot-tempered, the old warrior is respected by his men and feared by his enemies. Vitalstatistix himself has only one fear: he is afraid the sky may fall on his head tomorrow. But as he always says, 'Tomorrow never comes.'

Cacofonix, the bard. Opinion is divided as to his musical gifts. Cacofonix thinks he's a genius. Everyone else thinks he's unspeakable. But so long as he doesn't speak, let alone sing, everybody likes him....

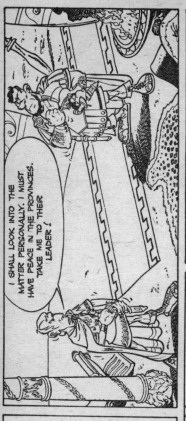

I KNOW, I KNOW... THEY STILL HOLD OUT AGAINST THE INVADERS. I'VE SEEN THAT SOMEWHERE BEFORE!

I SHALL LOOK INTO THE MATTER PERSONALLY. I MUST HAVE PEACE IN THE PROVINCES. TAKE ME TO THEIR LEADER!

¡HALT, ROMANS!

SOON AFTERWARDS...

AND YET THE NATIVES SEEMED QUITE INDIFFERENT TO OUR SQUABBLES

THEY WERE PROBABLY WAITING TO SEE WHO WON SO THEY'D KNOW WHO TO HOLD OUT AGAINST

PHEW! I BREATHE AGAIN!

SO I'M GOING TO HOLD MY BREATH UNTIL SOMETHING DOES HAPPEN TO ME

SO?

/ DON'T FORGET, O SPURIUS BRONTOSAURUS, IF ANYTHING HAPPENS TO ME YOU'LL ANSWER FOR IT WITH YOUR HEAD!

AND NOW WE'RE ALMOST AT TOTORUM! YOU WANT TO STOP AND PLAY! **NO!**

STOP! ALL RIGHT, WE'LL PLAY IT **YOUR WAY!**

HEY!

FORWARD, BOYS! AT THE DOUBLE!

WAIT FOR ME! HOW MANY TIMES DO I HAVE TO TELL YOU TO BEND DOWN WHEN WE GO OUT OF THE HOUSE?

O CHIEF VITALSTATISTIX, COME QUICK! THERE'S A FIGHT IN THE VILLAGE!

WHAT?

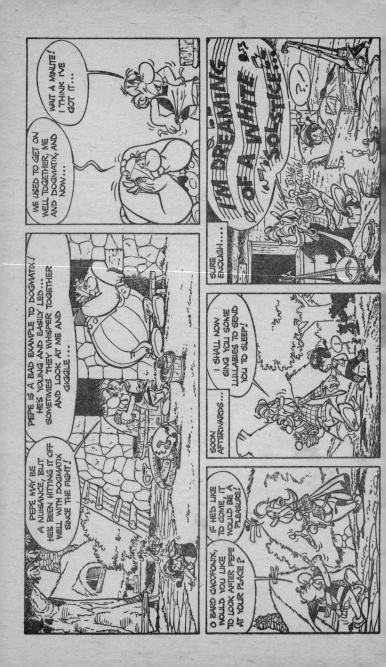

AND WHILE EVERYONE AT TOTORUM SEEMS HAPPY...

I SHALL SOON BE REJOINING MY GARRISON IN HISPANIA. I'M NOT NEEDED HERE ANY LONGER. THE GAULS KNOW THEY'RE BEING WATCHED. THEY WON'T MAKE ANY MOVE.

YOU CAN TRUST MY MEN! THEY DON'T GO BARKING UP THE WRONG TREE!

WE'RE NOT NUTS!

I SUPPOSE IT'S BECAUSE HE'S CLAPPED IN CHAINS

YES, IT WAS A CHAIN REACTION

...BACK AT ROME CAESAR'S TRIUMPH IS A HUGE SUCCESS, AND EVEN HIS CAPTIVE AUDIENCE CAN SCARCE FORBEAR TO CHEER .....

AND CAESAR, DELIGHTED BY THE APPLAUSE OF THE CROWD, MAGNANIMOUSLY SETS THE BARBARIAN CHIEFTAIN FREE

Capitol! Capitol!

TARAPPAPAPAF!

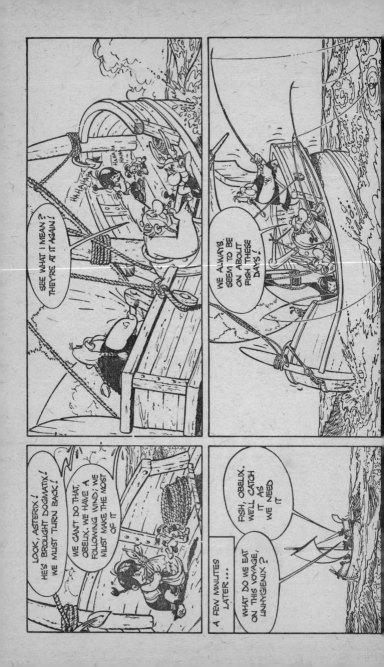

SOON AFTERWARDS...

BUT WHY ARE YOU ALL WAITING HERE?

IT'S THOSE ROMAN LEGIONARIES ON DUTY AT THE BORDER... THEY'RE HOLDING US ALL UP!

WHAT?!!! YOU CAN JUST GET IN THE QUEUE LIKE THE REST OF US! WE'VE BEEN CRAWLING ALONG LIKE THIS ALL THE WAY FROM *BURDIGALA!

* BORDEAUX

ROMAN LEGIONARIES?... LOOK, COULD MY FRIENDS AND I GET UP IN YOUR MOVING HOUSE AND...

COME ON! CAN'T YOU SEE WE'RE MOVING?

BELT UP! YOU'RE NOT INVADING US NOW!

COME ON!

THE LEGIONARIES WILL HAVE BEEN WARNED ABOUT US... WE'LL HAVE TO SLIP OVER THE BORDER SURREPTITIOUSLY

I'LL ASK THESE TWO LOCALS IF IT'S MUCH FURTHER TO THE TOWN

¿WINDMILLS? ¡CHARGE!

LATER...

IT'S HOT!

¡ I'M TIRED, ASTERIX!

WE MUST BE GETTING ON! GOODBYE, AND THANKS!

NO, IT'S NOT VERY FAR. KEEP RIGHT ON, BEAR LEFT AT THE WINDMILLS...

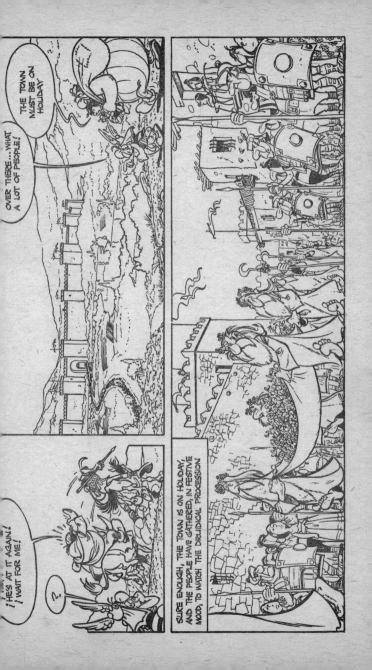

¡BUT HOMBRE, THIS WON'T WORK! ¡I HAVEN'T GOT ANY CARTWHEELS NOT TO GIVE YOU! ¡I'M RIGHT OUT OF STOCK! I'LL HAVE TO ORDER THEM, AND THAT TAKES TIME...

!?

AND HERE'S SOME MONEY FOR THE CARTWHEEL!

LISTEN... THERE ARE SOME PEOPLE OUT THERE WHO NEED A CARTWHEEL. I DON'T WANT YOU TO GIVE THEM A CARTWHEEL. IF THEY COME HERE, JUST TELL THEM YOU HAVEN'T GOT A CARTWHEEL.

OH, ALL RIGHT! I'LL GO ON MY OWN

NO, WE'LL ALL THREE OF US GO WITH PEPE!

FODDER STATION

CARTS REPAIRED

THIS IS MAD, WE WANT

OFF YOU GO, BOTH OF YOU! PEPE AND I WILL WAIT

AFTERWARDS...

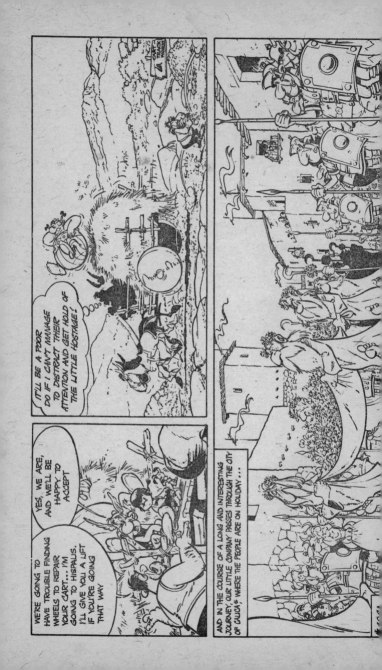

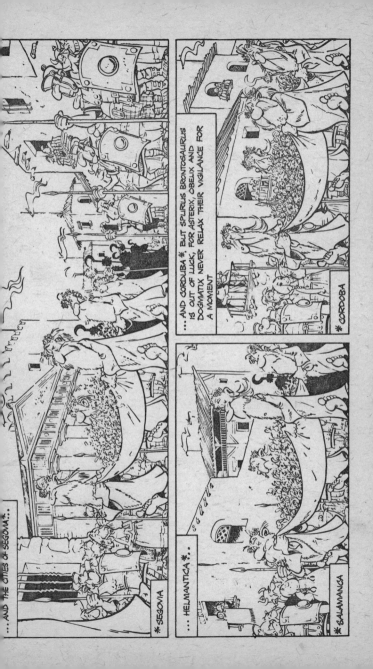